© 2011 Disney Enterprises, Inc.
Published by Hachette Partworks Ltd
ISBN: 978-1-906965-58-7
Date of Printing: May 2011
Printed in Singapore
by Tien Wah Press

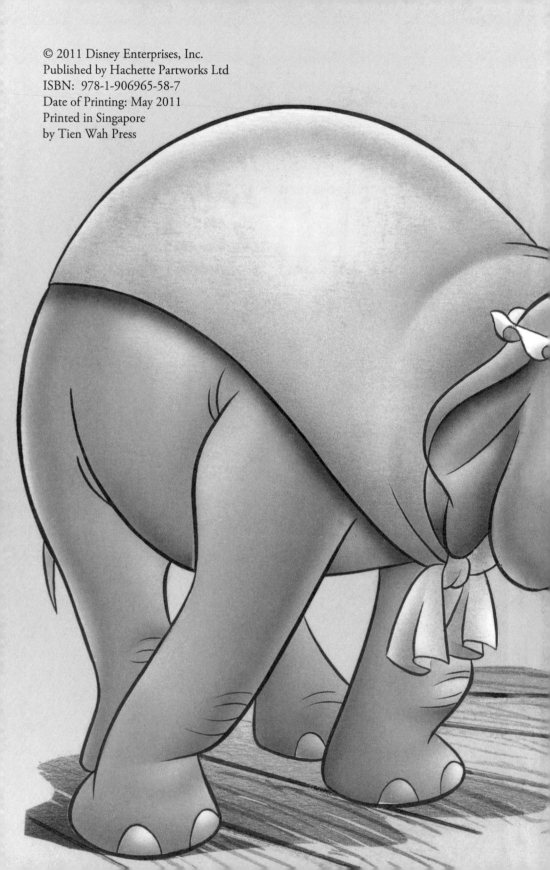

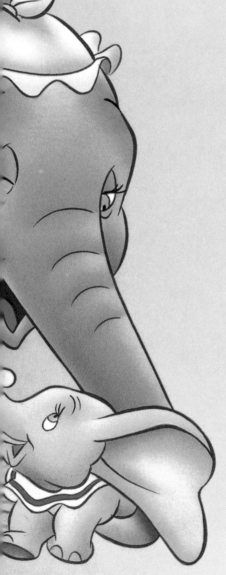

Disney

Hachette

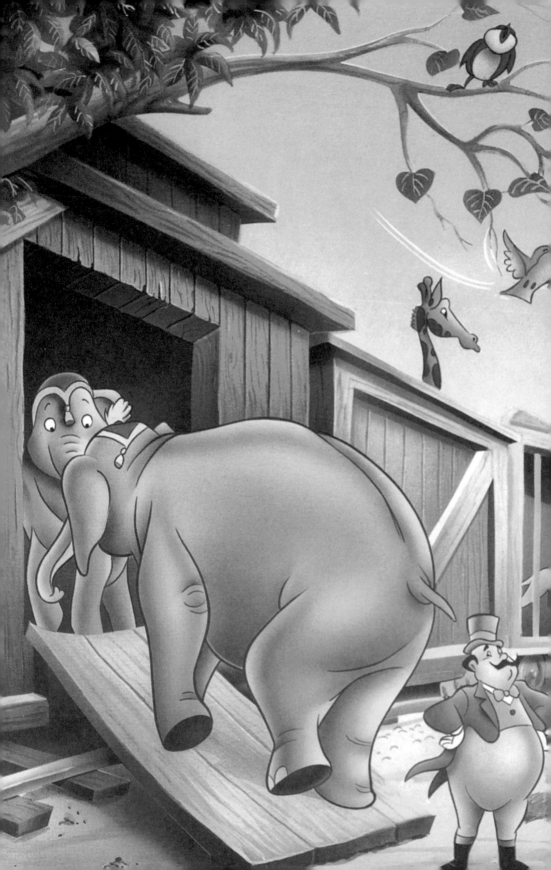

Spring had arrived. It was time for the circus to travel from town to town again.

Everyone was excited. But the most exciting thing about spring was still on its way.

Late one night, a flock of
storks flew over the circus
tents. Each stork carried a
special bundle.

The storks dropped the
bundles gently, because inside
each one was a baby animal!

The mothers were happy because their babies had finally arrived.

But one mother was not happy.

Mrs Jumbo waited all night, but there was no bundle for her. She took one last look at the sky before she got on the circus train.

"I hope my baby comes soon," she thought.

In the clouds above, one last stork was checking his map. He was trying to find the circus train.

"There it is!" he said. He grabbed the heavy bundle and flew off to the train.

"Mrs Jumbo?" he called. "Mrs Jumbo!"

"Over here!" cried all the elephant ladies. "Right this way!"

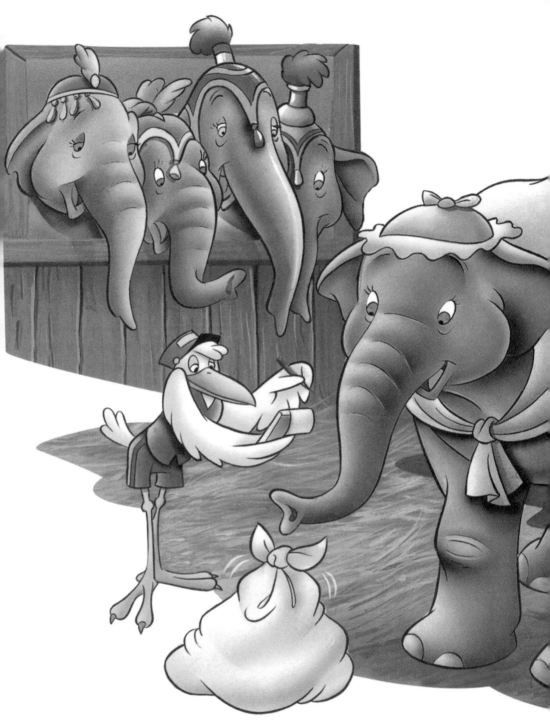

"Sign here please," the stork told Mrs Jumbo.

Mrs Jumbo was so excited! She couldn't wait to see her baby.

"Hurry up! Open it!" giggled the elephant ladies.

Mrs Jumbo untied the knot. Out
popped a baby elephant with
big, blue eyes. Mrs Jumbo
loved him at once.
Then the baby
elephant sneezed.
"AH-CHOO!"
Up flew his
enormous ears!

The elephants laughed at the tiny baby.
"What funny ears!" they said. "We will have to
call him Dumbo."

Mrs Jumbo didn't care. Dumbo was her baby, and she loved him very much.

Soon the circus reached the first town. Everyone had to help set up the tents – even the elephants!

The next day, the circus animals paraded through the town.

Dumbo tried to keep up with the other elephants. But he tripped on his ears and landed in a puddle! All the children laughed at him.

Later, some boys started to tease Dumbo and pull on his ears.

Mrs Jumbo rushed over to protect her baby. She gave one boy a spank.

"Help!" the boy cried.

The ringmaster heard the boy cry for help.
"Stop that elephant!" he shouted.
Soon, Mrs Jumbo was tied up and led away to
a cage.

That evening, the elephant ladies blamed Dumbo for everything. They wouldn't talk to him or even look at him.

Poor Dumbo! He missed his mother very much. Timothy the circus mouse felt sorry for Dumbo. He decided to teach the elephant ladies a lesson.

"Boo!" he shouted.

The elephant ladies screamed! They were all afraid of the little mouse.

Dumbo was afraid of Timothy, too. He hid
in a pile of hay.
Timothy offered the little elephant a
peanut.
"Don't be afraid," the circus mouse said.
"I like your ears. And I'll help you
get your mother back."
When Dumbo heard
that, he knew he had
found a friend.

As Dumbo and Timothy walked past the ringmaster's tent, they heard him talking about a new elephant act.

"I have an idea," Timothy whispered. He hurried into the tent.

Timothy was sure that once Dumbo was a star, the ringmaster would free Mrs Jumbo.

When the ringmaster fell asleep, Timothy whispered in his ear. "Your new elephant act will star Dumbo!"

"Dumbo... Dumbo..." the ringmaster repeated. Then he woke up. "I've got it!" he said. "Dumbo will be the star of my elephant act!"

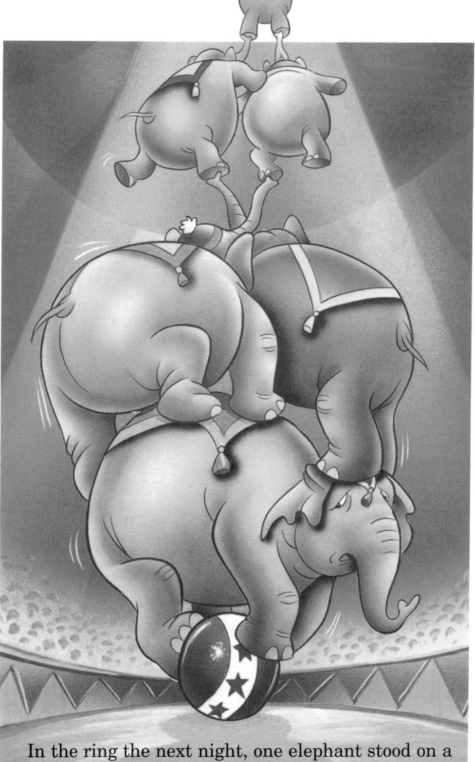

In the ring the next night, one elephant stood on a ball while the others balanced on her back.
"Stand still!" grumbled the elephant at the bottom.

At last, it was Dumbo's turn. He was supposed to bounce off a board and land on top of all the elephants.

Dumbo was very nervous when the ringmaster called his name. He ran onto the board and bounced...

... right into the ball. Dumbo had tripped over his long ears. CRASH! Down came all the elephants!

The people ran from the tent. Soon even the Big Top had crumpled to the ground.

The elephant ladies were very angry.

"That Dumbo doesn't deserve to be an elephant!" they complained. "He should be a clown!"

So the ringmaster
made Dumbo a clown.
    But the unhappy little
elephant didn't want to
be a clown. He had to
jump from a very tall
building into a tiny tub.

"Cheer up," Timothy said later as he helped Dumbo wash off the clown makeup. "We're going to see your mother."

Off they went to see Mrs Jumbo.

Mrs Jumbo heard them coming. She rushed to her cage window. Mrs Jumbo tried to see her baby, but a strong chain held her back. All she could do was stretch out her trunk to Dumbo.

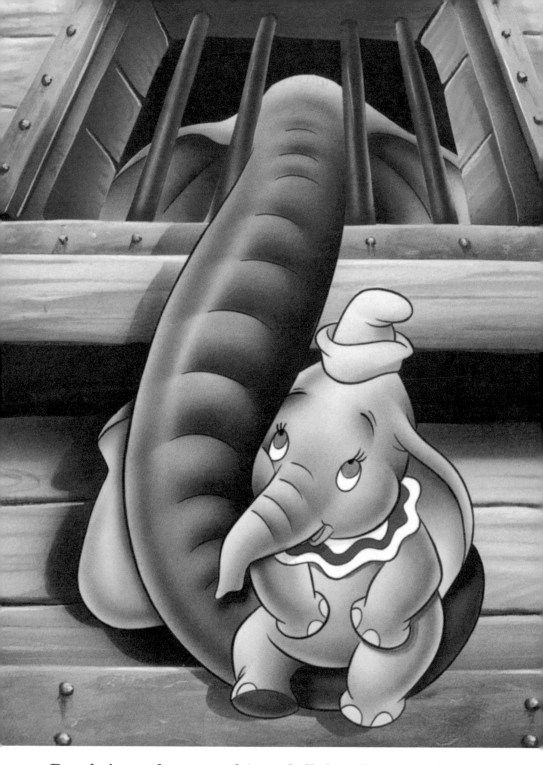

Dumbo's mother sang him a lullaby. He missed her so much! It was very hard to say goodbye.

The clowns were singing when Dumbo and Timothy returned. Dumbo had made their act a big success, and they were very happy.

But Dumbo was not happy. In fact, he got hiccups from crying so much.

"Drink some water," Timothy said. He didn't
know the clowns had made the water taste
funny. And the water made Dumbo feel funny.
It made him see two Timothys.

"What's wrong with the water?" wondered
Timothy. The mouse took a sip. The
water made him feel funny, too.

The next morning, a group of crows found some unusual visitors in their trees. Dumbo and Timothy were both asleep, high up on a branch.

"Have you ever seen anything like it?" they asked each other.

Timothy woke up.
"Don't look down,
Dumbo!" he cried,
hanging on tight.
But Dumbo looked.

SPLASH! Down they fell into the water.
The crows laughed and laughed. What a morning
they were having!

Timothy didn't think it
was funny.
"Go ahead and laugh!" he
said. "How did we get up
there, anyway?" he asked.

"Maybe you flew up!" cried the crows. They were only joking.

But Timothy jumped up and down. "Of course! Dumbo! You can fly! You can use your ears like wings!"

Dumbo didn't think he could fly.

The crows decided to help. They gave Dumbo a feather.

"It's magic," they told him. "It will keep you from falling."

They took the little elephant to the edge of a tall cliff.

Dumbo closed his eyes, flapped his ears and
jumped. The crows were right! He really *could* fly!
"Now we've seen everything!" the crows laughed.

"Wait until they see this at
the circus!" Timothy shouted.

That night, Dumbo
jumped from the
burning building.

But this time, he flew high over everyone's head!
Dumbo was a star! The ringmaster let Mrs Jumbo
out of her cage. Dumbo and his mother hugged
each other.

And nobody ever laughed at Dumbo's ears again.